Death Leap

by

Simon Chapman

Illustrated by Nigel Dobbyn

Published in 2007 in Great Britain by
Barrington Stoke Ltd
18 Walker St, Edinburgh, EH3 7LP

www.barringtonstoke.co.uk

ISBN: 978-1-84299-470-2

Printed in Great Britain by Bell & Bain Ltd

A Note from the Author

Last year I took my mountain bike on holiday with me to Cornwall. Near to my holiday cottage there was a bike trail that went all the way from the North Coast to the South Coast. The best bit was getting down to the trail which was in a deep valley. There was a set of old quarries with tracks that I would race down everyday and explore. One way led down a steep gravel slope then over an old bridge. There was a tunnel underneath.

I thought 'what if that bridge was broken – would I dare jump the gap?' I would be going fast enough. 'What if someone was chasing me – would I take the risk then?'

That was the 'Death Leap' that I built the story around – helped with extra ideas from some of the Year 11 boys that I teach at Morecambe High School in Lancashire.

For Hannah
– my feisty one!

Contents

Chapter 1
Witness!

Jake pulled his mountain bike behind a bush and waited. Some days he had to do this.

He'd drag the bike right up to the track at the top of the old stone quarry, and then there would be people there. If they saw him, they would shout that it was private land. At times they would call the police.

It was easier to hide. Jake would wait a bit and when the people had gone, he'd set off once more down into the quarry. He would speed down the track that he and his friend Chris had named the "Death Leap". There was the buzz you got from the first drop off and then the terror and thrill of the sharp edge that came next. It was simply the best run ever. And the most dangerous.

At the end came the famous Death Leap itself, but Jake knew he would pull out before that. Only one or two of the older kids had the nerve to make the leap, and Jake didn't plan to try it. He might well kill himself if he did. He was not ready for it yet.

This time there were two men at the top track. They were both wearing suits. They looked out of place. They were too smart. The men were standing next to a white 4 x 4. One of the men was handing a small

black case to the other. Jake thought he knew that man. Had he been in the papers?

This is going to take a while, Jake thought.

Safe in his hiding place, he pulled out his mobile and started playing with it, flicking through the photos in its memory.

He heard a motor-bike pull up. There was some shouting. Then he heard a loud bang.

It sounded like a gun but it must be the motor-bike's engine backfiring, Jake told himself. He peered over the bush.

The first man was pointing a pistol at the one Jake half knew. That man was now lying on the ground with a pool of blood spreading out underneath him. A third man in black leather gear was sitting on a motor-bike close by. He was looking into the black case, which was now wide open. For a moment, Jake just stared. It was like he was watching something on TV, but this

was real. Then it sank in. He had just seen a murder.

Jake knew he might be seen, so he ducked down behind the bush. He was shaking now. Should he hide here or make a run for it? He could call the police – but would they believe him? Unless – the thought popped into his mind – he took a photo! He pressed the buttons on his phone to switch it to camera mode. Then he poked it above the bush.

Ker-click. One more, just to make sure. He pushed the zoom function to get a better picture. Ker-click. Got it. He looked up.

"No!" he gasped. The men had spotted him.

Could he ring the police? No time! The man with the pistol was pointing it right at him.

"Get up. Show yourself!" the man shouted.

No way, thought Jake.

He crawled back to where the hill started to drop away. Then he ran with the bike. As he jumped into the saddle he heard a shot ring out. A puff of dust exploded on the path next to his back wheel.

Riding down the steep slope, the bike was moving faster. Soon he was under cover behind the wall of the quarry.

Chapter 2
Boxed In

Jake knew the best way to escape would be to go down through the quarry. He could get to the bottom and take the road that led back to town. But what next? He had been shot at once already. On the road, he would be an easy target. Even worse, he would be at the bottom and would lose his speed.

Jake checked his phone. No signal. He felt sick. He had to admit to himself that if he wanted to ring the police, he would have to go back up.

Jake skidded the bike to a stop and held his breath. Over the pounding of his pulse in his head he could hear the crunch of tyres on gravel. The 4 x 4. It was further down on the track, blocking him in.

He couldn't hear the motor-bike. This seemed odd. A bike like that could easily chase him down here into the main quarry. So why hadn't it? Most likely it was still at the top, in a place that would stop him going back the way he'd come.

Blocked front and back. There was only one other way out. Up. He would climb up the rocky sides of the quarry and drag his bike behind him. No problem – as long as he wasn't seen.

Chapter 3
Up the Wall

Getting up the first 20 feet wasn't that hard. The rock had been blasted out of the hillside in a way that left huge steps. Jake found he could push the bike up onto a ledge then climb up after it. There was no sound of a car below him now. But somehow he knew the man with the 4 x 4 was waiting there.

He thought for a moment how he could phone for help. He couldn't call 999 and risk being heard. No, he would text Chris with the photos. Chris would see them, understand the danger was for real and know what to do.

Jake stopped for a moment. He checked his mobile. Still no signal. He found Chris's number in the address book and got ready to send the first of the photos.

He was just starting to feel pleased with himself when he heard an engine.

Motor-bike. There could be no mistake. The sound was coming down into the quarry. Jake knew he had to move now. As the motor-bike shot into view, he swung his own bike up to the next level and pulled himself up after it. There was only one more section to climb. The biker was now below him. He was sitting on the saddle, revving and looking around. But he did not look up. Jake took his chance. He lifted his bike half-way up – but as he did so his phone tumbled from his pocket.

It sat on the ledge by his feet, half hanging over the edge. The smallest move and it would fall the whole way. The biker still had not seen him. Jake froze, his arms above his head, taking the full weight of his mountain bike. His muscles were in agony. He knew he couldn't last much longer.

Below him he heard shouting. It was not the biker but the smart man from the 4 x 4.

The killer. He was running into the quarry. Jake could see him taking aim at him with his pistol in a two-handed grip.

The man fired. At that same moment, Jake pushed the bike up with his left hand and swept his right one around to pick up the phone. He almost knocked it over the edge. The phone fell, but he grabbed it.

Beep! A signal. Jake pressed the send button. His message was away. Suddenly he felt he could do anything. He reached

above his head, pressed his finger-tips into a crack in the rock and pulled himself up.

Bang!

A bullet slammed into the cliff next to his arm. If he hadn't moved up at that very moment, Jake would have been hit. But this time his luck was in. He got to the grass at the top, pulled the bike to him and lay flat, out of sight.

For a few seconds he lay staring at the sky. He could hear the motor-bike below.

Soon it would get to him. Then – game over. He had sent the evidence. Now he had to stay alive.

A text message beeped onto his phone. Chris! Yes! His idea might just work.

Wll gt hlp. Sty thr :)

Jake laughed out loud. Stay there. As if that was going to be easy. How could he give two armed criminals the run-around long enough for Chris to fetch the police?

Then it came to him. As the motor-bike revved up the hill and into view he just had time to key in the words that only Chris would understand.

Death Leap

He pressed send.

Chapter 4
The Impossible Run

The Death Leap was the "impossible" run that Jake and his mountain biking friends had dreams of riding. Of all the ways you could ride down the quarry, this was the one that had it all – a steep drop at the start, jumps, and a narrow section which was like riding a knife-edge.

It ended with the Death Leap itself. Near to the exit to the quarry there had once been a bridge over the road. There was now a six-foot gap. Some boys had put down slates in the run-up to the gap to make a ramp so you could jump it.

But that wasn't all. Once you had done the jump you had to brake hard and skid left. That was the only way to miss going over a 20-foot drop just beyond.

Only someone who knew about that drop would know you had to brake. And that was what Jake was banking on. He would offer himself as bait and make sure the motor-bike rider came right behind him. The rider might be able to get over the jumps and down the knife-edge. (Jake hoped he would – that was the plan.) He might even be able to jump the gap in the bridge.

But would he know about the cut back that came right after that? Jake's real advantage was that he knew the track.

There was just one problem. Every time in the past that he'd come to that jump at the end, he'd bottled out.

Jake had never done the Death Leap.

Chapter 5
Tightrope Ride

As the motor-bike roared up the slope towards him, Jake sped off towards where the Death Leap run started. He was careful not to go too fast. For his plan to work, he needed the motor-bike to chase him. He knew that if he seemed to be too keen, the man wouldn't follow. So he rode down, not rushing and not looking back, until the engine noise was almost on him.

The motor-bike was only just behind and Jake knew its rider couldn't go back now. He had to follow.

Jake pulled his first stunt. He braked and at the same time hopped the bike sideways onto the steep slope to his left. Then he rode down, standing high off the saddle to let his legs act like shock absorbers every time he bounced on the hard ground. He was gripping the handlebars so tightly, that he could feel every bump through his fingers and sense if the bike was going the right way. More than any time before he had to keep the fear out of his mind and focus on the path ahead.

When he got to the bottom, he pedalled hard to keep his speed up so that he could jump a low bump in front of him. Then both the pedal bike and the motor-bike were speeding down again into the next level of the quarry.

The way was easy here. Any grass and weeds had long ago been worn down to mud on the "knife-edge" section. The motor-bike rider revved his engine and headed for the place where the track got really narrow, trying to head Jake off. Jake pedalled like mad and got there first. But now he had to slow down.

And that was almost the end for him. The motor-bike tyre clipped his back wheel. He nearly toppled over the edge. But the biker had made a mistake too. His speed dropped, and Jake got away. He reached the top of the final slope before the bridge jump. And waited. If ever there was a time to be confident about his skill on a mountain bike, this was it.

Jake, you can do it, he willed himself on. *But wait.* He checked himself. *The motor-bike has to be close or else the plan won't work.*

He stared at the man, eye to eye, as the other raced towards him. Jake knew the rider must not catch him. Then he looked down the slope and set off. The motor-bike,

just a bike's length behind, came after him.

Chapter 6
Death Leap

As he reached the slate ramp just before the gap in the bridge, Jake's mind was clear. His feeling of panic had gone. He would make the Death Leap or he would die. It was as simple as that. There was no more to think about.

His front wheel rode the home-made slate ramp, then for a moment there was nothing. The bike was silent. There was no shaking. There was empty space beneath him. Jake had time to take in the motor-bike taking off behind him – and the fact that a white 4 x 4 was speeding along beneath him.

His wheels hit the ground. Real life started again. Acting by instinct, Jake pulled his left brake to control the skid that now had him going sideways towards the cliff drop. He heard the motor-bike's engine – and its brakes screeching. Too late!

Jake saw the bike falling and its rider's leg bend backwards at the knee as he smacked into the ground.

One down, one to go, he thought as he pedalled down the last bit of the hill.

What happened next was too fast for Jake to take in. At the bottom of the slope the smart man from the 4 x 4 was standing with his pistol pointing at him.

I'm dead, thought Jake. *Just hit him!*

He rode right at the man, bounced off a rock and jumped the bike.

Chapter 7
Chain Set – Face Scrape

Later on, Jake would say he didn't know if the man had fired the pistol or not. All he could remember was the man's look of horror as the front wheel of the mountain bike came down on his head and then the chain-cogs scraped over his face.

Both Jake and the man went down. But Jake was faster to get back up. His arm was in agony and his side was badly scraped but otherwise he was OK.

The pistol was lying on the floor midway between them. Jake grabbed it and lobbed it away as far as he could. The stunned man was coming round now. Jake went to pick up his bike. He could see the handlebars and saddle were bent round; a five-minute job to fix, but he didn't have that time. He dropped the bike and ran. As he shot off towards the quarry entrance he

hardly heard the three police cars coming in.

They zoomed past him and screeched to a stop just short of the injured gangster. The man tried to make a run for it but two policemen tackled him. There were more policemen running towards Jake. And Chris was there.

Jake's head was spinning. Amazing – his plan had worked. Shaking with shock, he sank to his knees. He felt sick.

"Where's the second man – the biker?" one of the policemen asked him.

Jake pointed to the place where the biker had crashed.

"Are you all right, mate?" Chris came bounding up. "Jeez, Jake, they took one look at the photo you sent and they were off. It turns out the guy with the gun was a gangster or something. The man he killed was some factory owner. He was in the paper last week because his factory burnt down. I reckon he paid the gangster to do it but then something went wrong. What do you think?"

But Jake said nothing. He wanted to vomit. He felt dodgy. He got to his feet and spat the foul taste out of his mouth.

"You'll be a hero now, lad," one of the policemen said. "Two wanted criminals in the clink thanks to you."

"Yeah," said Jake. But he wasn't thinking about the gangsters.

Yes, he would be a hero now. The youngest person ever to have done the Death Leap.

Barrington Stoke would like to thank all its readers for commenting on the manuscript before publication and in particular:

Luke Berry

Jordan Brassil

Aaron Burrows

T. Cutts

Alun Davies

Josh Elliot

Sascha Edwards

Ryan Evans

Hoi-yee Fan

Taylor Foster

Luke Geary

Marcus Herbert

Ryan Hurst

Sinead Marie Isaacs

Marisha Kinjai

Connor Mortin

Sam Murren

Amber Lee Parnaby

Cadi Penny

William Probert

Laurabeth Sanders

Fiona Smith

Shane Snell

Emily May Sobey

Melissa Spencer

Holly Thomas

Nicola Thomas

Rhian Trevor

Samantha Watson-Shepherd

Become a Consultant!

Would you like to give us feedback on our titles before they are published? Contact us at the address below – we'd love to hear from you!

Email: info@barringtonstoke.co.uk
Website: www.barringtonstoke.co.uk

More exciting NEW titles ...

Kiss of Death
by
Charles Butler

Kate wants Nick.

Nothing will stop her

Not even *death* ...

More exciting NEW titles ...

Gremlin

by

Chris Powling

300 passengers.

One plane.

No pilot.

Can Glenn save them?

You can order *Gremlin* directly from our website
at **www.barringtonstoke.co.uk**

More exciting NEW titles ...

Shark!
by
Michaela Morgan

Mark knows about sharks.

But he doesn't know there's a hungry
shark out there, right now.

And it's coming his way ...

You can order *Shark!* directly from our website at
www.barringtonstoke.co.uk